Gracie's Angel

THE
LATTER-DAY DAUGHTERS
S E R I E S

Gracie's Angel
© 1996 by Launi K. Anderson
All rights reserved.
Printed in the United States

Library of Congress Cataloging-in-Publication Data

Anderson, Launi K.
Gracie's angel / by Launi K. Anderson.
    p.   cm. —(The Latter-Day daughters series)
Summary: In Salt Lake City, eleven-year-old Gracie
and her Mormon family experience hardship and loss
brought by World War I and the spreading influenza epidemic of 1918.
ISBN 1-56236-508-8 (softcover)
[1. Mormons—Fiction. 2. Influenza—Fiction.
3. Brothers and sisters—Fiction 4. World War, 1914-1918—Fiction
5. Utah—Fiction.] I. Title. II. Series.
        PZ7.A54375Gr   1996
        [Fic]—dc20   96-12976
                            CIP
                            AC

10 9 8 7 6 5 4 3 2 1

Gracie's Angel

THE
LATTER-DAY DAUGHTERS
SERIES

Launi K. Anderson

A S P E N
B O O K S

Dedication

To my children April, Lyndi, Jillian, Dane, and Rhen.
This love lasts forever.

Table of Contents

"Our families are not exclusively intended for this life. We live for time and eternity. We form relations for time and eternity. Our affection is prepared to endure not merely our mortal life—but throughout eternity."

Joseph F. Smith

People tell me that if something is real important you should write it down. That way you'll never forget it. I don't know if that's true or not, but I'm writing this now, not because I'm afraid of forgetting, but more because all I seem to do is remember.

CHAPTER ONE

Angel Morning

Gracie and I rode into town with Papa that first day. We passed the stores and shops that sat still and dark in the early dawn. No one spoke and only an occasional yawn broke the silence. We made it to Temple Square just after sunup.

Papa's regular weekday job was as the conductor for the south end trolley* running between State Street and Ninth East. The job  paid fair enough, but Papa was never one for sitting still, so he took odd jobs on Saturday. Sunday was always saved for the Lord.

This particular Saturday, though, was different from any other. "A once in a lifetime occasion," and Papa didn't want us missing it.

It felt so strange to watch Papa head toward the service entrance of the beautiful Salt Lake Temple wearing work clothes instead of his Sunday best. He acted uncomfortable, so I could tell he was feeling funny about it too. But like Mama had been saying all week long, "There was no way around, but through."

When the man at the door heard Papa say who he was and what he was there for, he laughed and said, "Yes, yes, Brother. Come right on in." Papa turned and waved good-bye to us and disappeared through the door.

Gracie and I walked back to the south side of the temple and found a good place on the lawn to sit. We wanted to be sure we could look straight up at the angel Moroni without staring into the sun.

It seemed to me like an hour before Papa appeared near the top of the main eastern spire* and stepped out onto the scaffolding.*

"There he is!" Gracie shouted, pointing upward. "He looks like an ant," she said. "I never thought anything could make Papa look small. He's half the size of the angel."

I nodded my head. "That's right. Papa told me the statue was nearly twelve feet high. This job won't be done today, that's for sure."

Gracie seemed troubled. "Papa's tall, but I can't see how he will ever reach twelve feet up."

"Gracie, the scaffolding's built clear up past the angel's head. Before he's done Papa will be looking straight into Moroni's face and touching up thin spots on top of his head."

Gracie smiled. She leaned back on her elbows in the grass, looking real thoughtful.

"I'm gonna do that someday," she said.

I squinted my eyes at her. "What? Gild* the angel? Can't you see how high that is? Why, no one would ever let a girl way up there."

She stared up at Papa working. "I don't care. Maybe I'll dress like a boy and fool them. I'm just saying that someday I'm gonna know what it feels like to be up there. I want to touch the face of that angel and look right into his eyes. Just like Papa's doing now."

"Well, Gracie," I said, "you let me know when it happens. I'm not gonna hold my breath."

Ever since she could speak, Gracie's been the one to have peculiar ideas. Oh, I don't mean peculiar-bad or anything. Just peculiar-different.

Like the time she sat outside all one day trying to figure out if birds fly through the sky or under it.

3

"What's the difference?" I asked her.

"Oh, there's a big difference," she said. "If they fly under the sky, I think that would be like sailing in a ship. But if they fly through it . . ."

She paused for effect.

". . . well then, that would be like diving into the sea. Only up, of course. Big difference, Jack. Big difference."

That's how Gracie looked at everything. Almost like she knew things the rest of us didn't understand.

She opened the large paper bag Mama had sent with us. Peering inside, she gave me the low-down on every morsel we'd be having for lunch. I reminded her that we planned to wait for Papa to come down before we started to eat.

"Oh, I know," she said. "I'm just looking. I like to think about my food for a while. Then I'm more in the mood."

I chuckled. "Whatever you say, Gracie."

I'm not sure what time it was, but it seemed like a lot of time had gone by when we heard a faint whistling sound. Looking up we caught sight of Papa waving his arm at us. We waved back.

Then something came floating from his hand like a tiny bird, gently making its way toward the ground.

"Look! Here it comes," Gracie said.

"What is it?" I asked. But she was already running over to where the small white paper was aiming to land.

I followed her, but whatever it was never made it down to us. Instead, it caught a breeze and floated over toward the temple roof.

"Darn it," Gracie said. She still looked up hopefully. "It must be stuck up there."

"What is it?" I asked again.

"Aw, nothing too great. Just a note. It was supposed to be a surprise for you. So much for that."

"Tell me what it said."

"Well, it doesn't matter now. Never mind."

I thought of pressing, making her tell me. But she changed the subject.

"Listen," she said, "Papa won't be down for a while yet. Why don't we go get a soda?"

I could see it was no use. I shrugged my shoulders.

That's another thing about Gracie. She always thinks up the best things to do. There's never a second to be bored with her around.

Every time I'd show up with a new friend from school or church, they'd ask me, "Why are you letting your baby sister tag along with us? Tell her to scram."

I'd usually smile and say, "Aw, it's okay. She won't be a bother. Anyway, she'll be twelve in December. That makes her only a year or so behind us. She's just small for her age."

I'd known for years what they'd find out real soon. Whether any boy was brave enough to say it out loud or not, being with Gracie was swell.

CHAPTER TWO

Brother's Keeper

Papa worked for a week on the statue. He ended up taking time off from his conductor job to do it. He said it was amazing to see how big the angel was when he stood face to face with it. Since it was only possible to work on small areas each day, it took longer than he'd figured on. His job was to sand, varnish, and re-gild the angel. We figure he was probably the first person to do it since the temple was dedicated.

One night at dinner, Gracie said, "Papa, what made them think that you could work on Moroni?"

He swallowed his food, looked at me and said, "Well, one day on my route, I heard a fellow telling another about the job. He said the hardest part of touching up the statue was finding someone who wasn't afraid of being perched a hundred and sixty feet straight up. And being the bold, adventurous, talented man that I am . . ." he winked at Mama, "well, I promptly asked for the job."

Gracie laughed. "How did you know what to do?"

"Dear," Mama said, "don't you know by now that there is very little your father can't figure out. He's what we call a jack-of-all-trades.* However," she gave him a stern look, "I would like the next job to be a little closer to the ground."

Gracie's face went all serious. "Papa, you were up terribly high. What if a gust of wind came and blew you off that scaffolding? You should have been tied with some kind of rope."

Papa tried calming her down by telling her about the safety harness he wore so that he wouldn't fall. But she kept on fussing about it.

"What if the scaffolding broke? There might even have been an earthquake or hurricane or something. What then?"

Papa made a silly face like he was afraid. "Gracie girl," he said, "if there had been an earthquake or hurricane, not having a rope would be the least of my troubles."

Speaking generally, Gracie isn't much of a worrier. In fact, most of the time she's too brave—for a girl, I mean. Unless it comes to Papa and me. I think she's got it in her head that she's supposed to take care of us, whether we need it or not. Whether we want it or not.

I remember a time she found a place that she was convinced would change our lives forever. Maybe it did. But at the time, the fellas and I didn't know what to think, but we followed her anyway.

She wound us in and out of trees, through a field, over a bridge until we ended up at the river. Then, after checking to make sure we weren't being followed, she led us to where the Chinese elm hangs its branches so far down they dip into the water. Stepping right in, she pulled the limbs back ever so slowly.

"Look at this," she said. Her voice sounded all mystical, like she'd found pirate treasure or something.

It appeared to me like an overflow channel* set in the bank, emptying mountain water into the river.

9

We all stood there staring at her.

Finally, I said, "It's just a runoff pipe. You mean to tell me we got our feet wet for this?"

"Oh, no, Jack," she said. "I've read about this at school. See where the water flows into the river? It forms a whirlpool."

"Yeah, so?" I was getting nervous that the fellas would think she was nuts. But I should have trusted Gracie.

"Jack, see how it's all hidden away like this? Don't you know what it is?

"Gracie, come on!"

"Jack, this is the legendary, long-lost fountain of youth!* Whoever submerges themselves in its waters will stay young eternally and live forever."

The guys laughed. But before any of us could say a word Gracie waded in up to her waist and walked carefully into the whirlpool. It was deeper there and she sunk to her neck. The current swirled and bubbled around her.

"Gracie, watch what you're doing," I hollered.

She put her hands up high and stepped into the flow. The channel runoff poured over her head. All at once she disappeared under the water.

I lunged forward, getting ready to pull her out.

But before I got to her, she popped up smiling like everything was just perfect.

"Gee whiz, Gracie!" I said. "You nearly scared the life out of me."

She sloshed right past like I wasn't even there. Then, reaching the bank, she faced us. Still grinning, she said, "Now, I'll be eternally young and live forever." Starting to head back home she turned, saying, "But don't you do it, Jack. It's too dangerous."

It's things like that. I mean, here we were, all of us nearly two years older and she's worried that we'll follow her lead. Sometimes it made me crazy.

We didn't tell her, but the next day, the fellas and I went to the fountain. For some reason, one by one we dunked ourselves in it. None of us ever knew why. We just felt we had to do it.

Now, Papa went in to his big chair and sat down with the newspaper, like he did every night. He folded it back, adjusted his reading glasses, and cleared his throat.

"Well, would you listen to this," he said. "Twenty-five German planes destroyed over Bulgaria." He turned a few pages. "And here's an updated Western Casualty List.* Uh-oh. There's a Utah boy in the severely wounded column."

Mama came in wiping her hands on her apron. "Oscar please, not war* news. Read us something good."

"Beating the enemy is good, Ruby. The sooner this war ends, the better off we'll all be. I've bought so many Liberty Bonds that I have more metal buttons than wood."*

"Did you get a new bond button,* Papa?" I asked. "You are still saving them for my collection, right?"

"Without a doubt, son." He reached into his coat pocket and pulled out a tiny steel button with a pin on the back. He flipped it to me, saying, "Here you go."

I held it up to the light. In bold blue print it read, "I BOUGHT MORE."

Papa picked up his paper again and said, "Now, what would you like to hear, Mother?"

"Whatever you read will be fine, dear. I just want the children to have more pleasant thoughts than the casualty list when they go up to bed. That's all."

"Of course you're right. Let's see." Papa flipped through the paper hoping to find something more cheerful. "Here we go. 'Lift off corns quickly and easily with Freezone.'" He looked up at us playfully.

We frowned at him pretending to be disgusted.

"No? Well, then how about this. 'Dobell's solution prevents influenza. Only thirty-eight cents a bottle. Now at . . .'"

Gracie giggled. "No, Papa."

Mama sat shaking her head. She found her sewing basket and took out the Red Cross projects she and Gracie had been working on for awhile. Last month the two of them knitted twelve pairs of mittens for the soldiers overseas. Now they were making socks.

"Here's one, Mother," Papa said. "Silk shirts at Z.C.M.I. Now I can just see myself in silk. Can't you, Ruby?"

Mama tried to keep a straight face and said, "Oh, yes dear. We'll have to get you one before the Queen's ball."

Everyone laughed except Papa. He acted shocked and sputtered, "Well, I never! All right then. This is my last try at satisfying you folks. It says here that the fair begins next week. The theme this year is 'Win the War.' I propose that next

Tuesday, the McBride family, being the patriotic souls we are, attend in full force."

Gracie and I stared at each other wondering if he knew what he was saying.

Mama beat us to it. "The children have school, Oscar. Remember?"

"Hang school," Papa said. "It says here that 'this event is not to be missed' and 'record number expected to attend.' Sounds like just the thing to brighten an autumn day. So for this one time . . . with your permission, Mother . . . school will take a backseat."

Gracie shifted her eyebrows at me and whispered, "Hot dog!"

CHAPTER THREE

Guardian Angel

We bolted into the fair at 10:00 Tuesday morning, missing school and all, like Papa said. Mama didn't like that much, but she went along with it anyway, saying, "This certainly isn't my idea of bringing up children responsibly."

He smiled at us when she wasn't looking. It was hard not to burst out laughing, but we knew better.

As I recall, nearly all of the exhibits were concerned with the war, in one way or another. There was one tractor display and a setup showing three new cookstoves. Luckily, the best part of any fair was the same each year. Food and goodies were everywhere.

We'd grown used to substituting syrup for real sugar in all our home baking (like the papers said, "War necessity demands it, Uncle Sam commands it!"). It was understandable then that Gracie and I were beside ourselves to see bags chockful of caramel corn, taffy, and cotton candy.

Papa was mostly interested in all the government booths. He aimed rifles, tried on combat boots, and studied warfront maps. Mama did her best to tug him towards more peaceful things, whether he was interested or not. She wanted him to take a look at the "War Garden, For Lot and Backyard." It showed plainly how any regular family could take a small space and produce their own vegetables on it.

But he just laughed. Papa, coming from a family of merchants, always considered himself too much of a "town-boy" to figure out how to get things to grow.

"Can you see us farming now, Ruby? Heaven only knows what would come up."

"Shame on you, Oscar," she said. "Even some of the elementary schools are growing War Gardens.* Now I know you find farming distasteful, but . . ."

"Hold on now," Papa said. "I never say anything against farming. I have always had the utmost respect for the industry and anyone involved. I simply cannot make it work for me. That's all."

"We should at least try it. Who can say? We might truly enjoy it."

Papa did a lot of chin scratching like he was seriously thinking about it, but we knew better.

Gracie picked up new Sammie patterns* for mittens, gloves, and something called a balaclava helmet* at the Red Cross booth. She kept really quiet that day, taking in all the sights without much to say about them—which was not like her.

I came up behind her and asked, "You okay, Gracie?"

"Oh, sure." She looked like she was far away, somewhere. "Just thinking," she said.

"Uh-oh. Anything but that."

She wrinkled up her nose and said, "Ha, ha."

Before the day was over, Papa, Gracie, and I snuck away and saw part of a horse race. That is, until Mama caught us. Of course we weren't doing any betting or anything like that, but she said the whole idea was disgraceful.

We took in two Vaudeville acts, an opera singer and a boy with a trick monkey. We saw a poster showing a man jumping from a tall platform into a tiny bucket of water. The sign said, "High Diver Dennis Tomorrow 1:30."

"Boy!" Papa said. "I don't want to be there for that one." Everyone laughed.

One exhibit claimed to have one of the oldest surviving original pioneers. His name was W. C. A. Smoot. He stood there showing all kinds of tools he had made with his own hands. He had a broom, a hammer, and a tin grater. We watched him grind corn with the grater. It took half an hour just to get a bowlful. I was sure glad we didn't have to do things that way anymore.

By four-thirty we were staggering around, entirely bushed. Gracie and I dropped the cores of our candy apples in the trash barrel on the way out of the fair grounds. She nudged me and nodded toward Mama and Papa holding hands as they walked. "Jack," she said.

"Yeah?"

"Things just couldn't get any better, could they? I wish it would stay like this forever."

I nodded my head and smiled.

Later that evening, while walking past her room, I saw her sitting on the window seat staring out into the night.

Stepping in quietly, I asked, "What'cha doing, Gracie?"

It took her a few minutes to collect her thoughts. Then, still looking out the window, she said, "Who is he Jack? Who is he, really? I know his name, but . . ."

"Who is who?" I asked.

"Moroni. Why is he the one on the temple? Why not Nephi or Mormon or Joseph Smith?"

"Beats me. It has something to do with him bringing Joseph Smith the Book of Mormon to restore the gospel. I learned about it in Sunday School. But I don't know the whole story."

"He sure is beautiful all lit up like that. I've always loved seeing the temple at night. When I was tiny, I remember Papa showing it to us from this window.

"He'd say, 'Right there, children. That's the closest place to heaven you can get, without leaving this world. And it's that temple that can keep us a family . . . forever.' Do you remember, Jack?"

I did.

"It's funny though," she said. "Even then, I used to think of Moroni as my angel."

I sat down by her and looked out the window. From her warm corner room she could see the whole glittering city. She was right, too. It was beautiful. The spires of the temple were a hazy glow in the darkness. But the angel . . . when the moonlight hit him just right he almost looked as though he were on fire.

"Since Papa worked on him," she said, "he's been more real to me than ever before. I like to think that he's watching over us. It makes me feel safer. Like everything is the way it's supposed to be." She looked up at me. "Does that sound strange?"

"No." I grinned. "It's just what I'd expect coming from you."

CHAPTER FOUR

Love Thy Neighbor

Mama and Papa left long before Gracie and I got out of bed. If they wanted to get a seat at general conference Mama said they'd need to be in line by daybreak.

Breakfast was still warm on the stove when we came down. I remember Gracie sitting across from me sprinkling cinnamon sugar on her baked apple, then pouring warm cream over the top. I take mine plain.

Between bites she said, "Did you hear about the Grangers?"

"Nope," I said. "What about 'em?"

"They're laid-up. The whole entire family. Even the baby." She took a long drink of milk, then looked up dramatically and whispered, "INFLUENZA."*

"You kidding?" I said. "Who's taking care of them?"

"I don't know. I heard Mama say it was serious business. She's planning to take in dinner tonight."

I sipped at my Postum,* thinking. It felt funny to be chatting over breakfast like two grown-ups. I took Papa's morning paper and snapped it open, then cleared my throat like he always does.

"Listen to this," I said in a low voice. "'King Ferdinand Abdicates Throne.'" I flipped the page.

"'American Forces Crush the Huns.'"

"'Does American red blood course through your veins? Prove it! Buy Forth Liberty Loan Bonds.* Help our Sammies* win the war.'"

Gracie bit her toast pretending to be Mama. "Oh, no Oscar. Not war news. Think of the children."

"Sorry, my dear," I said, trying not to laugh. "Here's one. 'Z.C.M.I. 50th Anniversary Sale. Coming soon. Watch for it.'"

Turning from the paper I said, "Be sure to pick the children up a few new toys, Mother. They've been so good."

Gracie covered her mouth, but laughed anyway.

Caught up in my great audience, I started

reading faster. "'Victrola Records announces two new tunes out by Caruso and DeLuca.'

"'Lydia Pinkham's vegetable compound brings relief to thousands.'

"'Influenza Spreads Across State. The deadly . . . illness . . .'" I stopped reading aloud. We weren't smiling now.

Gracie sat straight faced. "Go ahead. Read it, Jack."

I took a deep breath and held the paper up closer to my face. "The deadly illness is moving across the state of Utah. Ogden reports sickness is leaving its mark as the death toll rises daily. Outbreak first reported on October 3rd. Hospitals filled to capacity while Spanish Influenza is rapidly spreading across the nation."

Gracie sighed. "The poor Grangers. I wonder if they have any family that will come and care for them."

"I don't think so. Aren't they from back East somewhere?"

"That's right." Gracie clicked her tongue like she does when her thinking cap is on. "Let's help them. You and me. Let's take them dinner like Mama wanted to."

"I don't know, Gracie. We aren't sure what Mama was going to do. Maybe we should wait for her to come home."

"Come on, Jack. How hard could it be? Besides, Mama and Papa will be tired when they get back. What do you say?"

I always have a hard time arguing with Gracie. And when I do, I'm usually sorry.

"Oh, all right," I said. "But you're making the soup. I do not cook."

It surprised me to see how well Gracie got around the kitchen. Sure, I knew she helped Mama all the time, but I didn't think that meant she could do it all by herself. We cut and boiled chicken, vegetables, and rice. Then we made egg noodles and set them aside to dry. She dropped the noodles into the steamy broth and I stirred slowly. The soup smelled so great that I started to feel sorry that we were giving it all away.

"Why didn't we think to make twice as much?" I asked. "Then we'd be all set for supper, too."

Gracie said, "Mama doesn't have a stew pot any bigger than this one. That's why. Anyway, we can always make another batch."

It made me tired to think of it.

Gracie carried a large tray with a basket of rolls and I came behind with the steaming kettle of soup.

As we reached the neighbor's side porch, she held her hand back towards me.

"Wait," she said. We walked around to the front of the house and saw a man hammering a large paper onto the door. It read in big black letters, INFLUENZA. In slightly smaller print below it said, QUARANTINE.*

"Oh no," I whispered.

"What's that supposed to mean?" Gracie asked.

The man turned to us and said, "That means, young lady, no one in or out of this house, unless it's the doctor. And that's me. You best be running home."

"We brought some supper in for the family," I said.

"So that's what smells so good," he said.

Gracie just stood there not saying a word.

I said, "Yes, sir. Chicken soup. We thought it might help."

"Well, you never know. That was mighty kind of your Mama. Here, let me take it in. You two best

25

get yourselves back now. You don't want to catch what they've got in there." He pointed toward the house with his thumb. "Hear me?"

Gracie still didn't answer.

I said, "Yes, sir," and handed the soup up to him.

Walking up our path I said, "What's the matter with you? You in some kind of trance?"

Gracie's face was all frowny, and I thought for a moment she had tears in her eyes. Stopping dead in her tracks, she blurted out, "So the Grangers just have to stay in their house? Until when? How will they take care of the baby? And if what they've got is so catchy, why isn't the doctor afraid of getting it?!"

"Golly, I don't know! Why you hollering at me?"

She sighed real loud and said, "Sorry, Jack. I just don't like things sneaking up on us like this."

I felt like putting my arm around her, but I didn't want her thinking I'd gone soft or anything. "They'll be all right," I said. "You'll see."

She looked back at the Grangers' house. "I sure hope so."

CHAPTER FIVE

Heat Rises

A week or so after taking soup to the Grangers, we noticed five or six other quarantine signs posted on houses up and down the street. The Relief Society sisters checked with the families in our ward regularly to find out who was sick and who was well. Many families who had several people under the weather* needed help with firewood or meals.

If a mother or father was down, the children were farmed out* to healthy families, so the patient could be nursed back to health. If it was a bad case, or there was no one to care for the sick person, they were taken to the hospital. Our neighborhood was lucky. With so many people willing to help, there were only a few who ended up at the hospital.

Gracie heard Papa tell Mama that Mr. Ancona the baker and a girl from our school had actually died. We didn't talk about that, though. Gracie and I found ourselves speaking in whispers whenever influenza was mentioned, as if to say the words out loud would bring us bad luck.

One morning we came downstairs all dressed and ready to make the trek to school.

Papa looked up from his breakfast and said, "Why, you two look slick as a whistle. What a shame to waste all this beauty by cooping you up here at home."

Neither one of us said anything at first. We both just turned to Mama to see if Papa should be believed. She stood with a look on her face that was hard to describe. Like she wanted us to be happy about it, but she wasn't.

I spoke first. "What's going on? Are we really staying at home?"

Mama nodded. "It appears so."

"Why?" Gracie asked. "I know the fair is over. So it can't be that."

"No, it's not that," Mama said. "Your Papa read a notice last night from the state health officer. Until further notice, all public gatherings are banned. It seems the influenza outbreak has become a full-fledged epidemic."*

Gracie sat down on the stairs. "So what does it mean 'all public gatherings are banned'?"

"Well," Papa said, "lately, anytime people have gotten together in crowds, more than half of them have gone home and taken sick. The health officials hope that by keeping everybody away from each other, the illness will stop spreading. What it means is no visiting other families, no school, no meetings."

"Not even church? Really?" Gracie asked. "But I have the Sacrament Gem* this week."

"You'll just have to say it for us," Mama said. "Our family will hold Sunday School right here at home."

I'd never heard of anything like this before. Quarantine was designed to keep sick people from being near healthy ones. But this seemed like locking up people who were well just like they had already taken ill.

Gracie looked worried too.

Papa reached over and tugged on her pigtail. "Come on you two, cheer up. You ought to be acting like kids who've just gotten a vacation from school. It won't be so bad."

Mama said, "I have a list of projects from the Red Cross that we can work on together. But this time they are for the hospitals, not the soldiers."

29

"But first," she took out a folded newspaper page from her pocket, "we need to understand a few things about influenza."

"Awww," I groaned. "This is going to be worse than school."

"Hush up, Jack. I want to hear it," Gracie said.

Mama tacked the page from the *Deseret Evening News* on the wall next to the stove, then began reading it to us.

RULES TO COMBAT FLU*

1. Avoid needless crowding—Influenza is a crowd disease.

2. Smother your coughs—others do not want the germs you throw away.

3. Your nose not your mouth was made to breathe through—get the habit.

4. Remember the three C's—a clean mouth, clean skin, and clean clothes.

5. Try to keep cool when you walk and warm when you ride and sleep.

6. Open the windows always at home at night; at the office when practicable.

7. Food will win the war if you give it a chance. Help by choosing and chewing your food well.

8. Your fate may be in your own hands—wash your hands before eating.

9. Don't let the waste products of digestion accumulate. Drink a glass or two of water on getting up.

10. Don't use a napkin, towel, spoon, fork, glass or cup which has been used by another person and not washed.

11. Avoid tight clothes, tight shoes, tight gloves—seek to make nature your ally not your prisoner.

12. When the air is pure breathe all of it you can—breathe deeply.

The minute Mama finished reading, Gracie and I ran in and washed our hands twice, clear up to our elbows. That done, we loosened our shoelaces and began breathing deeply. Mama made us stop when Gracie started getting dizzy.

The first job she and I were given was to sort through the old bedsheets and table linens. Any with moth holes or frayed edges we put in a pile. The good ones went back into the closet. Mama said she wasn't sure if the old linens would be used for bandages or compresses or what. But the nurses needed them to help the flu patients in the hospital, somehow. Papa was in charge of collecting spare blankets from our neighborhood and taking them to the Red Cross station.

The strangest thing of all was that if we went outside, especially if we'd be around anyone else, we had to wear white gauze masks. That way, we could keep our germs to ourselves. Papa read to us about a barber from Ogden who was fined ten dollars for refusing to wear one. It felt silly at first, but we soon got used to it.

Late one afternoon, I found Gracie sitting outside on the porch looking up at the mountains.

I sat down by her and said, "Where are you now, Gracie?"

She looked up and smiled. "Not so far away, really. I was just thinking. Everything is happening so fast these days. The war was bad enough, but now with the flu everywhere, I feel like . . ." she turned her head away so I couldn't see her face.

Sitting forward I tried to look at her eyes. "What?" I said. "You feel like what?"

"I just wish our lives could stay like they've been. But I don't think they will. That's all. I just don't think they will."

"Well, I'm not planning to change. And Mama and Papa will always be the same. So what are you worrying about?"

She rubbed two fingers across her eyes.

"Hey, Jack, I have a question for you."

I nodded.

"If it's true that heat rises, then why is there snow on top of the mountains but not the bottom?"

I grinned at her. "Well, one thing we can count on. You'll always be the same."

CHAPTER SIX

Flu Sunday

"Okey-dokey, family," Papa said. "What song shall we sing?"

Gracie and I just looked at each other. This 'Flu Sunday School' as Papa called it, was new to us, and it was hard to keep a straight face.

The General Sunday School Board had actually come out in the newspaper and given instructions on how to hold church meetings at home. Papa was taking it very seriously. He told us we were to:

1. Gather our family at 10:30 A.M. on Sunday.

2. Strictly obey all Board of Health rules.

3. Teach a gospel lesson.

He asked again, "Does anyone have a favorite song?"

Gracie raised her hand as if this was real school. "How about 'Love at Home'?"

"Good choice." Then nodding toward the piano, Papa said, "Mother, would you be so kind?"

Mama sat down on the bench and searched the Church hymn book for the proper page. She had trouble getting it to stay open, so I sat by her and held the corner. I figured that way maybe no one would notice if I wasn't singing.

Papa stood to lead the music. He raised his arms like there was a choir in front of him. But when he realized Gracie was the only one there, he stopped short.

"This will never do," he said. "Gracie, sit on the other side of your mother."

She hopped up like she was in the army. "Yes, sir!" she said.

"And Jack, I know what you're thinking and it won't work. We'll expect the tenor part from you, loud and clear. Mother can you manage to still play while flanked* by the youngsters?"

"Yes, dear."

Mama began the introduction while Papa stood at the side of the piano with his arm raised again. We started out low, but got louder with a few well placed nudges from Mama.

> There is beauty all around, when there's
>   love at home.
> There is joy in every sound, when there's
>   love at home.

Peace and plenty here abide, smiling sweet
　　on every side.
Time doth softly, sweetly glide, when
　　there's love at home . . .

We finished all four verses, and it was over none too soon for me. Though, I must say, we'd gotten quite good by the end.

Mama gave the opening prayer and sat back on the sofa.

Papa made the announcement that even though we would not be having the sacrament, a Miss Gracie McBride would still bless us with the Sacrament Gem.

Gracie stood, pinched out the sides of her dress, and curtsied.

"This isn't a play, Gracie," I said. "It's supposed to be church."

"Shhhhh!" Papa said, making a stern face at me. "Forgive that outburst, Miss. Please continue."

She batted her eyes at me then held up a piece of paper. I guess she decided she didn't need to look at it, because she put it back down, and said, "Sacrament Gem, October, Nineteen-eighteen. 'In remembrance of thy suffering, Lord these emblems we partake. When Thyself Thou gavst an off'ring, dying for the sinners' sake.' I say these things in the name of Jesus Christ, Amen."

Papa gave a lesson called the widow's mite. He said that Jesus taught about a very poor woman who donated a tiny amount of money to the church. Even though it was not much in the eyes of the world, it was a great sacrifice because it was all that she had. He was an interesting teacher and we learned what a mite was. Gracie said she was happy to find out that it wasn't a bug. Even Mama laughed at that. I knew Gracie was only joking, but it was funny.

Mama played "O My Father" for the closing hymn and we sang without laughing this time. Before I gave the prayer, Papa made one more announcement.

"When we are through here, I hope you will all pitch in and help your Mother with dinner. She has prepared a lovely pork roast with potatoes and gravy. And as a special surprise to you, we will be having . . ."

Gracie and I held our breath hopefully.

". . . now, now," Papa said. "Try to maintain your composure, family. As I was saying, we will be having CHERRY PIE for dessert. Jack, if you will, please."

I stood and gave the prayer, remembering the sick, our soldiers, and a blessing on the food.

After dinner, like every Sunday I could remember for years, Papa read to us as he sat back in his easy chair. Gracie and I had probably been too old for the stories shortly after we started school, but it didn't matter.

Papa found the children's corner in the paper and began reading the "Little Stories for Bedtime." That afternoon the title was "Billy Mink Learns His Lesson." The very best part about the stories was lying on the floor on our stomachs listening to Papa make up a new voice for each character.

Reddy Fox, Billy Mink, and Jerry Muskrat were silly animals and thank heavens the stories were never very long. Before one was ever finished, though, Papa would get mixed up about what voice he was using for who. We'd be laughing so hard that sometimes we never got to the end at all. It's not something I'd ever tell the fellas, but Sunday at our house was a great day.

CHAPTER SEVEN

Fare Thee Well

"Papa, don't leave," Gracie said.

I heard her voice so early in the morning, it startled me. I came downstairs, half asleep, trying to figure out what was happening. Gracie looked sad and tired standing there hanging on to Papa's sleeve.

"Gracie, let go now," he said, real quiet. "I'll be just fine. The whole state is crying out for volunteers. Somebody's got to help. The hospitals are full to overflowing and I need work."

Papa's conductor job had been cut back. The health board could only allow fifty people on the small trolleys and seventy-five on the large, so not as many people tried to ride them anymore. With the new crowd limits* people stayed home more often. When his work stopped being steady, Papa had to look for something else to make up the difference in pay.

Utah State University had set up as a temporary hospital for returning soldiers who had the flu. They were in desperate need of help and Papa was eager for work, even if it meant taking a risk. There was a nationwide call for nurses, but people were afraid of catching the flu, so anyone who was willing to help was hired on the spot.

Gracie tried again. "I'm just so afraid something will happen to you. What if you catch it from one of those soldiers? Papa, please wait for a safer job to come along."

"Honey, listen to me," he said. "Sometimes there are just things a person knows they are supposed to do. You've felt that way before. Like when you had me take that note up the temple spire."

"It didn't do any good," she said. "It never even came down."

"That doesn't matter. It did you some good. The point was to feel like a piece of you had been up there. Whether or not Jack got the note makes no difference.

"Now, I need you to understand something. President Smith has asked us to help each other every way we can. You would have me obey the prophet, wouldn't you?"

Gracie nodded.

"Now, I feel I'm needed at this hospital. I don't know why. I may never know why." Papa pulled Gracie to him. "But you, my dear, must be strong and let me go."

Maybe she understood because she just has "feelings" about things herself, but something Papa said truly struck her. She looked up at Papa and stepped slowly back. The worry was gone from her face.

I came downstairs so Papa could kiss us all good-bye. He walked down our path and turned to wave again.

"Good-bye family," he called. "Take care of each other. I'll be back soon."

Gracie, Mama, and I stood at the open door until Papa was out of sight.

"He really will be all right," Gracie said. It was like she was talking to herself. "It's not him."

"What did you say, Gracie?" Mama asked.

She just shook her head and said, "Nothing."

As I recall, it was days before Papa came home again. He left word with our neighbor that it wouldn't be until week's end. When he did come it was nothing like we'd expected.

Gracie sat in the front room sewing when a loud rap on the window made her jump. She hopped off the couch and stood in the doorway.

"Mama!" she called. "Someone's out in our yard."

Mama came in from the kitchen. "Good heavens! Who could it be? Jack, you and Gracie go lock the doors."

I took the rear door and Gracie turned and grabbed the key from the front. We came back in time to see Mama moving the curtain. She stepped closer, then quickly slid the lock and threw the window open. A light snow was falling, but she poked her head outside anyway.

"Oscar! Whatever are you doing out there?"

Gracie and I looked at each other and without meaning to, said together, "Papa?"

Mama talked quietly at the window while Gracie fumbled with the key in the front door. She swung it open, but before we could make it onto the porch, Mama turned.

"No, children," she said. "Come back. Close the door. Your Papa won't be coming in."

We knelt on the couch so we could listen to Papa through the window. He stood there getting covered with snow.

"And how are my two youngsters?" he asked.

"Papa," I said, "why aren't you coming inside?"

"Been too close to the action, the doctors say. They think I'd be taking a big risk waltzing into my own home. I was only allowed to come here by promising I'd stay outside. And what a fine night I chose to do it, I might add."

"Tell us about the work you do, Papa," Gracie said.

"When I first got there," he told us, "I mostly stayed with the heavy jobs that the nurses couldn't do. But just yesterday they had me moving beds . . . and patients."

"Oscar, do be careful," Mama said.

"Oh, I shall. Never you fear."

After telling him everything we could think of about our week, we gave him a few moments to talk to Mama alone. Gracie and I went into the kitchen to make him some warm cocoa. We came back to the front room and leaned out the window to hand it to him.

"Ahhh," he said. "This will thaw me right out."

Mama gave him a sack loaded with clean clothes, dried fruit, and a loaf of cinnamon bread.

He twitched his mustache and shook his head, scattering snowflakes everywhere.

"Whew! I need to head on back. I can see if I stand here very long, I'll be a permanent fixture in the yard."

We couldn't help laughing. But it was hard to see him go. He blew us all kisses and winked at Mama, then turned and walked off into the night.

I thought about the families all over the world who had been sending their brothers and fathers away to the war, not knowing if they'd come back.

"I wonder if this is how it feels to send a soldier off," I said.

"Naw." Gracie smiled. "'Cause we know our Papa will be back."

CHAPTER EIGHT

Wounded Bird

Mama was convinced that Gracie took a chill by the window that night. When she came down to breakfast the next morning she looked peaked* and pale. She picked at her cornflakes and never once put the spoon in her mouth.

"Gracie, what's wrong?" I asked. "You look terrible."

She smiled weakly and said, "Thank you, Jack."

Mama came in and put a pan of biscuits on the table. She dropped the potholder and came around to where Gracie sat and felt her forehead.

"Honey, you're burning up." She turned to me and said, "Jack, help me get Gracie back to bed."

Mama put her arm around her and tried to lift Gracie up from her chair. I could see Gracie had little strength in her legs. A surge of panic ran through me, but for some reason I didn't move.

"Jack!" Mama said.

I'm ashamed to say that even then, I was too afraid to do anything.

Gracie looked up at me. She knew I was scared.

"Don't be afraid, Jack. It'll be all right," she said. "I'm just feeling a little tired."

I whisked around the table and scooped her up like she was a wounded bird. Gracie, like I said before, has always been small for her age, but it still shocked me to feel how light she was.

I made it upstairs and laid her back in her bed. Mama sent the neighbor boy for the doctor. He couldn't come until the next morning.

The doctor confirmed what we feared. Gracie had the influenza. She had it bad. The doctor ordered quinine to break the fever. Sage tea, he told us, would loosen the congestion. She was to be massaged with Vicks VapoRub and wrapped with a flannel scarf. Before he left, he opened the window in her room as high as it would go and told us to keep the fresh air coming in. For the first time in my life, I felt a chill in Gracie's room.

We piled on quilts to keep her warm, and she slept.

For the next few days she'd be with us one moment and far away the next. Mama warmed a tiny pan of olive oil and used hot packs to soothe the fearful pain in Gracie's ear. Her cough became deep and tight.

I came upstairs after stoking up* the fire and recognized the sour smell of mustard plaster.* The doctor was just coming out of her room.

I heard him tell Mama that whenever there was an influenza sign on a door, it became the responsibility of the parents to send any healthy children away. Anywhere, for their own sake.

He barely got all the words out before I exploded.

"You're not sending me anywhere! I'm not leaving! Mama needs me, and Gracie needs me. Do you hear what I'm saying?!"

Mama rushed over and grabbed a hold of me. "Jack, Jack. Stop it," she said. "The doctor is only doing what he thinks is best."

Turning back to him, she said, "I'm sorry, Dr. Stone. Forgive my son. This has been terribly hard on him. He and his sister are very close."

"Yes, yes," he said. "I understand. But for his own health . . ."

Mama broke in, "I appreciate your concern, Doctor. But with my husband away, Jack is truly indispensable to me. I feel it would do all of us more harm than good to be separated."

He just nodded and walked back down the stairs. Before he left, he told Mama that he would be less concerned for Gracie if her cough were stronger. He told her that the worst part of this epidemic was when the flu led to pneumonia.

"That's the real killer," he said, wearily.

There was no need to send Gracie to the hospital since she was getting better care than she ever could there when they were so crowded. I was relieved to hear that no one would be trying to take her away.

I went up and sat by her bedside. She looked so tiny and frail that it frightened me. I stood very still, watching and waiting for  her to breathe. In that moment I realized how empty everything seemed without her odd questions and happy chatter.

Taking hold of her hand, I stroked the back of it with my thumb. I used my other hand to wipe at the tears burning down my cheeks.

Outside Gracie's window I saw the light on her angel Moroni glowing down from the temple spires. It was as if her voice filled the room.

"I like to think he's watching over us."

Oh how I wanted it to make me feel safe, like she said it made her. But it was hard to feel anything while she lay there so still.

I buried my head in the warm quilt folded over her.

"Don't leave us, Gracie," I cried. "Please don't leave us."

CHAPTER NINE

Falling Star

I'm not sure exactly when the sickness hit me.
I awoke in the night with thunder crashing
through my head and fire burning down in my
chest. From my chair, I looked to where Mama sat
asleep in the rocker at the other side of Gracie's
bed. I closed my eyes, trying to ease the pain that
blurred my sight. There was a dull ache with every
breath I took.

Gracie! I thought. *What about Gracie?* I slid my
hand sideways and moved the quilt where she'd
slept. To my horror I realized she was no longer
lying in the bed. As I slowly raised my head I saw
her standing at the open window. The freezing,
November wind blew her curls gently back.

I tried to stand, but was overcome by dizziness.

"Gracie," I whispered. "What are you doing?"

She turned and smiled at me, then looked back
out the window.

"I was just wondering," she said in a soft, tired voice. "When a star falls from the sky, do you suppose the night gets a bit darker?" She looked back out the window. "I think it must. Don't you, Jack?"

I tried to nod, but couldn't.

She took the blue afghan from the foot of her bed and wrapped it around my shoulders. Slowly, she climbed back into her bed and pulled the covers up around her. I felt her shivering. She tenderly laid her hand on my arm.

"Don't worry, Jack," she said. "Everything will be all right. It isn't you."

I couldn't make sense out of what she was saying. I felt as though the darkened room was spinning around me, and all her words were flying past. If only Mama would wake.

Cold. It was so cold. The only warmth was Gracie's hand on mine.

Papa, where are you? I thought. *We need you.*

In my dreams Gracie and I ran through tall grass and rode streetcars and drank sodas together. Her fountain of youth poured over our heads as we laughed and splashed in the spring thaw, knowing we would now live forever.

She ran ahead of me, faster and faster. I struggled to keep up, but she was getting farther and farther away. At last she stopped. When I reached her she stood still, pointing. I shaded my eyes to look up, up to where the angel on the temple spire glistened in the sun. Gracie was walking away from me.

"Stop, Gracie. Stop," I tried to say.

"I love you, Jack," she called. "I love you."

She was gone.

I awoke to the sound of Papa's voice saying my name. I opened my eyes just for a moment, to see if he was real or just part of my dreams. He was crying. I felt his hands on my head, warming me, making me safe.

He lifted and carried me out into the cold.

My sleep was restless. I seemed to be racked by chills one minute and fits of coughing the next. As hard as I tried to force my mind to work, to think, to remember, it was no use.

Even the smells were strange and disturbing. The blanket that kept me warm was not mine. Noises I'd never heard before scared me.

I felt a very hot and very bad-smelling cloth on my chest and struggled with all my might to move away from it. I used whatever strength I could gather to thrash around. I wanted the burning cloth off of me.

Suddenly someone was taking my hand and squeezing it gently. I heard a whispered voice say simply, "Lay still, Jack."

I forced my eyes open, just enough. Gracie! She sat on a wooden chair at the side of my bed. Her face was full of color and she looked well!

I tried to speak, to tell her how happy I was that she was stronger, better, and most of all, with me. But all I could do was smile.

She smiled back.

For the next while, each time I opened my eyes, she was there. She held my hand, touched my forehead, and told me over and over that I must be strong. That I must get well.

I had no idea how long I'd been sick or in the hospital or, for that matter, how long I'd been asleep. But I wanted to get better, for Papa and Mama and for Gracie. If she could do it . . . so could I.

One morning I woke to the sight of my parents at the end of the bed. A doctor was talking to them, about me I suppose. I couldn't hear what they were saying, but for the first time in a long while, I was curious.

My throat felt so dry that when I tried to talk nothing happened. I couldn't believe I was so weak that to even move my arm was nearly impossible.

I swallowed hard and cleared my throat. Everyone turned. For a moment they just stood and stared at me. Then both Mama and Papa rushed to my side.

"How do you feel, son?" Papa asked.

"Water," was all I could say.

He put his arm behind my back and helped me sit up. Mama held a tin cup to my mouth, and I sipped slowly. My lips were cracked and sore with fever blisters. The water tasted so good. I closed my eyes and laid back against the pillow.

"Not again," Papa said in a playful voice.

I opened my eyes and grinned at him.

"Honestly, son, three weeks of bedrest should be enough for anyone."

I looked around the room. Had I really spent three weeks in this hospital room? Nothing looked familiar to me except my parents. I turned my head slowly, taking it all in. To the right of me stretched a long room with other sickbeds exactly like mine. On my left were two more. Sitting snugly up against the wall was a wooden chair. *The* wooden chair.

"Gracie," I whispered.

Papa came closer. "What's that?"

"Where is Gracie?" I asked.

Mama put a trembling hand over her mouth and held onto Papa's arm.

His eyes glistened. "Jack," he said slowly, "You were so sick. You couldn't know. Gracie is . . . Gracie is gone."

"What?" I whispered. "What do you mean, gone?" It was as if they were speaking another language.

"Son," he said, "I came as soon as I heard Gracie was sick. When I got home I found you, burning up with fever sitting beside her bed. Brother Granger and I administered to you both, but Gracie was nearly gone when I got there. It was as if she was just waiting for me to come."

I turned my face away. "But she was just here," I said. "She sat in the chair. She held my hand."

Mama and Papa stood staring at me.

I started to cry. I felt like I was falling and unable to catch myself. *Gracie couldn't be dead,* I thought. *She'd been here to see me. She told me to be strong. Why, I might not have fought so hard to live if she hadn't . . .*

Mama came to my side and stroked my hair. Her chin quivered as she tried to tell me it would be all right.

I struggled to sit up. "That's what Gracie told me. It would be all right. She said, 'Don't worry, Jack. It isn't you.'"

Papa looked over at Mama and a strange understanding seemed to light their faces.

I covered my face with my hands and sobbed.

Papa said, "Son, I think maybe Gracie knew she was being called home."

Wiping at my eyes I said, "What do you mean? How could she?"

"Well, you know how she was. She lived her whole life like she knew a secret that the rest of us didn't. And she said something to me, right after the blessing, that until now I didn't understand. As weak as she was, she looked right up into my face and said, 'Don't worry, Papa. It's me.'"

He put his arm around Mama and struggled to speak.

"She knew, Jack. And she was trying to help us understand so that we could let her go."

They hugged me and we all cried.

She did know.

CHAPTER TEN

LOVE FOREVER

It was months before I was strong enough to go out. When we did go, I didn't care. Everything was too quiet, too sensible, too solemn. I wanted to be caught off guard by some nutty question. I wanted a reason to laugh. I wanted to stop feeling alone in a room full of people.

Getting over influenza was nothing compared to trying to get along without Gracie.

It was about mid-March when Papa came bounding into the house and announced that he was taking us all on a drive downtown.

"Enough of this gloom," he said. "Son, I believe we are expected to live on, even with the pain."

I smiled at him and nodded.

The sun felt warm on my back. It was a perfect day for a recovering invalid. We drove straight down South Temple where Papa stopped the car. "Everybody out!" he said.

At first, I thought I'd fold up and die going back to Temple Square . . . without her. Everything would surely remind me of something she said or did. But to my surprise, as we came through the gates of Temple Square, I felt calm.

We went inside the Assembly Hall first, and Papa told us all about the great pioneers who built it. We peeked through the Tabernacle windows and wondered how many people it would take to fill it up.

At last, we mustered up enough courage to walk up to the temple itself. I didn't feel like I thought I would. I felt warm and peaceful.

I asked Mama and Papa if they'd mind me walking around to the other side by myself. They understood.

It took half a second to find the exact spot where Gracie and I sat that day and watched Papa work. I looked up to the beautiful gold angel standing there holding his trumpet.

I closed my eyes and remembered Gracie saying how she was going to touch the face of that angel someday. She didn't care how high it was. She was going to do it.

"You sure were something, Gracie," I said to myself.

Just then a strong gust of wind whipped past, which made me pull my jacket a little tighter. I wondered if now Mama and Papa would want to hurry home for fear I'd catch a chill. I turned to see if they were nearby. Off to the side of the temple I notice a white piece of paper fluttering around in the breeze. It reminded me of the mysterious note Gracie had tried to send me from this very spot. It floated down slowly as if it had no intention of ever truly making it to earth. But somehow this one did. It landed near the very bush Gracie had run to that day, in the hopes that her own paper would fall right into her hands.

I watched for a few minutes as it swirled and lifted, only to see it finally land in the flower bed at my side. I tried to ignore the impulse to pick it up, but it got the better of me.

I reached into a clump of pansies and took out the yellow, tattered paper. Unfolding it I tried to make out the writing. The words were faded but still readable.

It said:

WHEN YOU THIS GOLDEN ANGEL SEE
I HOPE THAT YOU'LL REMEMBER ME.
WITHIN YOUR HEART I'll ALWAYS BE
AND NEVER WILL GO FAR FROM THEE
LOVE FOREVER,
GRACIE

The words seemed to jump off the paper as I read. My mouth dropped open. I looked up again to the temple spires. Clutching the paper in my hand, I tried to believe what had just happened. Looking at the note one more time, I slid it carefully into my shirt pocket.

The one just over my heart.

JACK'S GLOSSARY

balaclava helmet (pg. 17)—A knitted cap that is made to cover the head and neck. It is meant to be worn under a soldier's hard helmet.

bond button (pg. 12)—A small, metal button with a pin on the back. They were given out by the banks to encourage people to buy more war bonds. People wore them to show that they were helping the war effort by buying the bonds.

crowd limits (pg. 39)—During the influenza epidemic the health board ordered that only small groups of people could ride on trolleys, take the train, or be in a building. Because the health hazard was so much greater when crowds gathered together, people were sometimes fined up to fifty dollars for breaking this rule.

epidemic (pg. 28)—A disease that spread far and wide very quickly.

farmed out (pg. 27)—Being sent to a neighbor or relatives house until it's safe to return home.

flanked (pg. 35)—Coming up on the right or left of something. In this case Mama.

Forth Liberty Loan Bonds (pg. 22)—A certificate that shows that you loaned the government some money to use to help the war effort. If Papa bought a bond for $18.50, in a few years it would be worth $20.00.

fountain of youth (pg. 10)—In school Gracie read a legend about a great fountain that would make a person young and give them eternal life if they swam in it. Many great explorers, such as Ponce de Leon, spent their lives looking for this fountain.

gild (pg. 3)—Papa replaced the tiny layers of gold called gold leaf wherever it was worn on the statue. The process is called gilding.

influenza (pg. 21)—A sickness that gives a person coughing pains and a fever. Most of the time the flu just makes you sick. But the epidemic of 1918 was a strange one because it was deadly.

jack-of-all-trades (pg. 8)—When a person is handy at a lot of different jobs he is called a jack-of-all-trades.

mustard plaster (pg. 47)—A poultice-type treatment made of dry mustard, flour, and hot water. It was smeared on cloths and laid on the sick person's chest to break up congestion.

overflow channel (pg. 9)—A pipe that carries water to another place.

peaked (pg. 45)—Pronounced peak-ed. When you don't looked so good and everyone can tell that you're sick.

Postum (pg. 22)—A toasted grain and molasses drink, served hot. Many people enjoy it as a harmless substitute for coffee.

quarantine (pg. 25)—Keeping a person away from others to keep from spreading a disease or illness.

Rules to Combat Flu (pg. 30)—The health department felt that these guidelines would keep people as healthy as possible. We have since learned that some of these rules were not helpful and some were even unwise. For instance, we now know that leaving a window open in a sickroom, especially in winter, can lead to pneumonia.

Sacrament Gem (pg. 29)—A short scripture or verse recited just before the sacrament in opening exercises of Sunday School to set a spiritual mood.

Sammie (pg. 22)—The American soldiers during World War I were nicknamed Sammies after Uncle Sam, a symbol of patriotism.

British soldiers were called Tommys. I don't know why.

Sammie patterns (pg. 17)—Knitting and crocheting instructions for making things the soldiers needed such as mittens, or socks.

scaffolding (pg. 2)—A platform made to hold people who are building or repairing something.

spire (pg. 2)—One of the six points on top of the Salt Lake Temple. The front three represent the First Presidency of The Church of Jesus Christ of Latter-day Saints. The back three represent the Presiding Bishopric of the Church.

stoking up (pg. 47)—Piling up more wood and coal to make a fire burn hotter and longer.

trolley (pg. 1)—An electric bus that runs on tracks. Before electricity the trolleys or streetcars were pulled by mules.

under the weather (pg. 27)—Feeling sick.

war (pg. 12)—From 1914 to 1918 many countries of the world were at war. The Allies—France, Britain, Russia, China, America, and many other countries—fought against the Central Powers—Austria/Hungary, Bulgaria, Germany, and the Ottoman Empire. Before the war ended over ten million troops were killed and much of Europe lay in ruins. The Allied forces won the war.

war garden (pg. 11)—During World War I everyone was encouraged to grow as much of their own food as they could because many things were being rationed. People turned their backyards in to gardens and many schools turned their playgrounds into gardens all to help the war effort.

Western Casualty List (pg. 11)—A list appeared in the newspaper almost every day announcing the names of soldiers who had been wounded or killed.

wood button (pg. 12)—Most of the buttons on clothes we wear are made of wood or rolled leather.

What Really Happened

During the years 1918 and 1919 nearly one fifth of the world's population suffered from the Spanish Influenza. More than 21 million people died, including 675,000 Americans. It is believed that World War I soldiers returning from the front brought the deadly virus home and infected millions.

In Utah, general conference, war victory parades, and the holidays all contributed to spreading the virus across the state. Public gathering was banned, while quarantine signs hung from thousands of doors. With over 2,300 deaths, Utah had the second highest death rate from the disease in the country.

Though no documentation is available to either prove or disprove the claim, it is believed that John Henderson Kirby, an LDS immigrant from Glasgow, Scotland, re-leafed the statue of the angel Moroni sometime between the years 1913–1919. It is possibly the first time it was gilded since the dedication of the temple.

About the Author

Launi K. Anderson was raised in Los Angeles and San Diego, California. She worked for a large local bookstore for four years and became the children's book buyer. She loves historical fiction and enjoys the research as much as the writing.

Her favorite things are: Thanksgiving, flutes, autumn leaves, ballet, cats, and old photos.

Launi lives in Orem, Utah, with her husband Devon, their three daughters, and two sons.

More about
The Latter-day Daughters Series

After reading Gracie's story be sure to enjoy the other books in the Latter-day Daughters Series. They are about girls just like you who lived in other times and places. Read about Violet, who helped settle St. George; Clarissa, who had to leave everything to come to America; Anna, who was a special friend to the Prophet Joseph Smith; Esther, who celebrated Utah's statehood; Sarah, who played matchmaker for her father; Maren, who cared for Joseph and Emma Smith's children; and Ellie, who celebrated the 50th year the Pioneers entered the Salt Lake Valley.

Watch for many more stories of adventure, laughter, tears, and fun. They have been written just for you!

From *Marciea's Melody*
Another exciting new title in
The Latter-day Daughters Series

Suddenly I was very angry. The roots of my hair seemed to be burning.

Samantha touched my arm, but I moved away from her and right into Sandy's face. "What is wrong with you, anyway?" I asked.

"What's wrong with *me?*" Sandy asked. "I'm not running around town with *her.*" Sandy stuck a finger right in Samantha's face.

Boy, if I had been Samantha, I'd have bitten that finger right off.

"Check in the mirror, Marciea," Sandy said. "You two are not the same color."

The Latter-day Daughters Series